# Watching

# Watching

## Scottish Short Stories

by

*Edith Buchanan*

DIADEM BOOKS

**Watching: Scottish Short Stories**



Published by Diadem Books
Distribution coordination by Spiderwize

For information, please contact:

Diadem Books
16 Lethen View
Tullibody
Alloa
FK10 2GE UK

www.diadembooks.com



ISBN: 978-1-908026-38-5

For Julie, Ruth and Edith

# Contents

# Foreword

AFTER THE DEATH of my husband in 1999 I found that writing was a great source of solace. My first attempts were based on memories of growing up in rural Scotland. The early stories are embroidered autobiography dated approximately 1935-1947. Later as I became more confident I drew on wider ideas.

My purpose in putting some of my work into book form was to give my family a glimpse of how different life was, especially the pace of life.

I wish to thank tutors and colleagues who encouraged me when I faltered and patiently listened to all my attempts. The writers groups at the Harbour Arts Centre, Irvine, have been my mainstay. Without their unstinting appreciation and encouragement this publication would not have been possible.

*E.B.*
September 2011

# Watching

**JINNY LIKED VISITING** her Aunt Peggy's. Now four years old, she was allowed to go by herself over the field to the farm. The trouble was the bullocks. You never knew when they'd put their heads down and make a sudden breenge. Mammy had said to mind and watch them, so she skirted the field, keeping close to the hedge. High up she could see the reds of the hips and haws against the deep blue sky, and through gaps in the hedge the turnip field with the purple turnips sitting up straight in rows. She had learned how to make turnip colour. She had drawn a picture of them and rubbed white on top of the purple, and then some yellow mixed in as well. When her big brother Davy had lifted turnips from the field for Hallowe'en lanterns, she had shouted at him, 'Find the biggest, the fattest and the roondest, Davy. I want tae hiv the best lantern!'

That night she'd get begun making it. She would dig out the turnip with a spoon. That would be sore. Davy was good with his knife though; he'd help her. She climbed over the stile into the loan. She was safe now, and began running fast until she was puffed out. As she rounded the corner of the farmhouse she saw her Uncle Sandy's bright red van sitting in the yard. On its side in big gold letters was the sign: *ALEXANDER McKAY FAMILY BUTCHER.* She knew that because Auntie Peggy had taken her finger and drawn over the letters, spelling it out. She was coming out of a shed carrying a big white basin, and had been feeding the hens.

'Have yi collectit the eggs the day?' Jinny asked.

'Och aye, a while ago. Ah'm gaun tae get on wi ma bakin' noo.'

Jinny would stay then. Auntie Peggy always gave her a hot scone.

'Whaur's Uncle Sandy then?'

'He's in the byre.'

'How?'

'Because he's busy.'

'Whit's he daein?'

'This is killin' day.'

'Whit kind of killin'?'

'Killin' the bullock.'

Jinny wondered what kind of killing that could be. Her black cat had killed Davy's white pigeon. The white feathers with the red blood on them had lain scattered all over the back green. Davy had been roarin' and greetin' and hittin' her, saying it was her stupid cat and her fault. Mammy had had to stop him from hurting her badly.

'Auntie Peggy, can Ah watch the killin'?'

'Ah don't think yir Mammy would like that.'

'She's no' here; she cannae see me. Ah'll get my wee stool.'

She carried the stool from the kitchen and dumped it down in the middle of the yard.

'Ah'll jist sit here and Ah'll can see fine.'

She watched the farm cat rolling on its back on the warm stones, and then she saw her Uncle Sandy coming into the open shed. He had on his butcher's overall the same colour as a tea biscuit, and he had put on his wellington boots. He was walking backwards, leaning well back, pulling a thick rope. His hands were big and red like his face. His bunnet was pushed up at the front and he was sweating. At the end of the rope was a big black ring through the bullock's nose. Its head was stretched out and swaying, low down. The ears stuck out sideways just like her black woollen mittens.

The wild staring eyes were like Davy's brown glass marbles. Snotters and slavers hung down to the wet floor, and as Uncle Sandy heaved, the beast's legs sprachled on the slippy flagstones. She saw her big cousin Archie had come to help. He was pushing at the bullock's backside. And then Uncle Sandy took a toy gun like Davy's and stuck it at the side of the bullock's eyes. The eyes stayed wide open but its legs couldn't hold up its big body, and it slid down, turning on its side. The legs still tried to walk but not for long. Archie handed a silver pail to his father, who lifted a shiny knife and cut a hole in the bullock's throat. All the blood came pouring out at once and filled up the pail. Then he began to cut at the neck and sawed a line right down the middle of its black, wet skin. Jinny remembered her box of crayons at home with the red and yellow, and her favourite purple colour she had used for the turnip shapes. The farm cat meowed and curled round her legs. It rolled over in the sun and began to wash its face with long, clean white paws, over and over and over. The colour of its fur was the same as the tablet Mammy had made for Hallowe'en. She could smell Auntie Peggy's baking coming from the kitchen and she wanted to go home now.

'Jinny! Come awa' in noo. You've sat there ower lang. Come and get your scone, lassie.'

She handed the scone to Jinny. The yellow melted butter oozed out under the red jam which dripped onto her black shoe.

'Ah'll jist awa' then, Auntie Peggy.'

'We'll see you for your Hallowe'en, Jinny. Ah hear you're comin' oot wi the big bairns.'

'Aye, Ah'm tae get oot this year... A cannae wait!'

She took the long road home by the loan, not wanting to see the bullocks. The scone in her hand was cold and she knew she couldn't eat it. When she got to the back door she flung it into the hens' pail, burying it in the brock with the long wooden spurtle.

'Is that you, Jinny? Yir back awfu' early, dearie.'

'Can Ah get on wi ma Hallowe'en mask an' ma turnip lantern?'

'Wait till efter yir tea and yir Daddy'll gie ye a haun.'

Jinny and Davy were dressed up and ready for the guising. They were waiting for their cousins Archie and Hector before they set off round the doors to beg for their Hallowe'en. There was the smell of cooking turnips coming from a pot on the fire. Rowed up on the table the lanterns with their crudely-cut faces had been lit, the soft yellow candle-light filling the kitchen. Davy had coloured his mask green. Ruler-straight lines radiated from blank eye-sockets.

He still wore his grey school pullover and had tied a tartan scarf round his middle.

'Daddy! How dae yi like ma mask? Ah'm the man that can see through wa's!'

'Laddie, yi hae an awfu' imagination. Ah doot yiv been readin' ower mony books.'

Jinny tugged at her father's jacket.

'Daddy, Daddy! Will Ah fricht a' the folks d'yi think?'

'Oh aye, yi will that.'

Her mask was roughly cut. Davy had helped her with the eyes but she wouldn't let him use the red crayon for the cheeks—just white. In her tight fist she had held the white crayon and scored layers of haphazard lines, impatient to be finished.

'Tie ma string, Davy. Ticht. Tichter!'

Her fair curls, now pushed high on her head, shone in the candle-light. An old white flour-bag covered her slight body; her legs were thin black sticks poking out at the bottom of it.

'If it wasnae for yir mask, Jinny, yir mair like an angel.'

'Naw, Daddy, Ah'm no an angel, Ah'm a bogle! Ah'm a bogle, d'ye hear?'

There was the sound of the sneck lifting on the back door in the scullery.

'Wheesh. Jinny, that's the boys noo!' shouted Davy.

'Quick, get ready tae gie them a fricht. Come awa' in and show yirsels.'

There was a snorting and bumping and the door was flung open.

A great roaring filled the kitchen. Archie had fixed a fankled hank of black wool to his head between two cow horns. He had coloured the whole of his face with cochineal, and round his body he had wrapped an old bit of black tarpaulin.

And then the screaming began.

'Jinny, Jinny! It's Erchie. He'll no hairm ye. He'll no touch ye!'

Rigid with terror she flattened herself against the wall, still screaming.

* * *

The fire in the room had died down. Carried on a rising wind there was the distant barking of a farm dog. Blatters of rain on the window drowned the soft hissing of the Tilly lamp. On the table the sagging skins of the dead lanterns distorted their gaping, smoke-blackened eyes and mouths. The remnants of the Hallowe'en costumes still hung over the chairs. At the back of the box bed Jinny lay asleep in her mother's arms. Her fair curls were darkened and flattened with sweat, and around her brow ran a scarlet line where the string had cut into her fair skin. Her father, seated at the table, lifted his head and looked over at them. He couldn't get the sound of her screaming out of his mind.

'Ah said, that bairn'll need watchin'. She'll aye hae the wind in her face. Aye, she'll need watchin' a' richt.'

# Hear the Music

**IN ISOBEL'S FAMILY** bikes were passed on to them like old clothes. The clothes were in a better state than the bikes with their rusty frames, flat tyres and worn brake blocks. Isobel free-wheeled. This bike was running smoothly. She hadn't been too happy about the basket at the front. The minister's wife had one the same. Still, it had come in handy in her plan and she liked the bell. The bell's ring had a sweet peal. When sounded it merged with the tune which had been running in her head like a fever all week. It had begun in the music class when they opened their books at a new song—'Come Back to Sorrento'. While the others had straggled round the melody Isobel had mouthed the words:

*'Hear the music of the waters,*
*Sounds of tender passions sighing.'*

Her mind had been far away after Roberta had whispered, 'That's where Mario comes from. Mammy says he's the best Tally worker they've ivver had on the farm. He's a great singer an' a'. Have yi heard 'im? He's aye singin' in the fields.'

Isobel smiled to herself. She had lain on the back green

listening to his sweet tenor voice floating over the fields. For days she twirled round the stations on the wireless searching for a voice that sounded like Mario's. When she found it, it went on and on and she wished it would never stop. After it ended there was a long shushing noise and she thought the battery had gone dead again. But it had been people clapping, then cheering and shouting Bravo! Bravo! As the class droned on she decided she would learn the song off by heart. She wouldn't sing it but whistle it to Mario while he was waiting for the Tally lorry. When she'd finished he would shout Bravo, just like on the wireless and in Italian—what's your name? Ah Isobel, bella Isobella—how wonderful you are, whistling the song of my Italy, my beloved home, my family, and you are so beautiful with your long fair hair, let me touch it... and she'd slide along the wall and sit up close to him.

That evening she had searched through her atlas for Italy. Italy, Italy, she had shivered when she found the page. Lovingly she traced its shape down the back of the heel, along the foot, round the toe and up—where was it? Oh joy! There was Naples, and finally in small, small letters—Sorrento. Leaning forward, she had kissed the grubby page tenderly. Her plan could begin. The whistling would be easy, but she knew that no matter how long she spread herself like a cloth laid out on the green to bleach, her legs would never be sun-tanned like the film stars'.

Now she could see the church clock and must hurry. In the distance the Tally lorry was groaning as it began its steep climb from the bottom of the brae. Isobel felt more excited than when the school bus had whined and stuttered to a halt in a snowdrift. Everyone had cheered and spent the day sledging. Before the last run down into the village she braked to a sudden stop at a farm gate. From her basket she lifted a paper bag and flung it into the field. She heaved herself over the gate and behind the hedge took off her skirt, jersey and socks. Frowning, she shoved her pale legs into a pair of khaki shorts which her brother had worn to his scout camp, then folded up the legs until they jammed against her thighs. Rolling up her socks, she stuffed first one, then the other under her vest against her thin flat chest, and pulled the belt with its metal buckle as tight as she could bear. Gathering up her clothes she noticed a clump of primroses blooming on the shady bank. She could hear the words again, from Mario's song:

*'Naught can set my heart a-beating*

*Like the fragrance of its bloom.'*

Gently she picked two of the delicate flowers and placed them in the pocket of her blouse. Already she could see their creaminess against Mario's brown hand. Back on her bike, she remembered her hair. With one hand she tugged and freed her long fair pleat, letting it stream out behind her as she gathered speed. Ahead she could see Miss Turnbull. She had forgotten she would have to pass her house. In her cottage garden Miss Turnbull weeded, clipped and raked every day from morning till night. Isobel thought she was the most boring person in the world, and put her head down.

In her green flowery overall, her arm outstretched holding a bunch of pink roses, Isobel thought she looked as if she was playing at statues all by herself. Usually she would call out, 'Don't yodel—you'll spoil your sweet voice,' or 'Ladies don't whistle, Isobel.' But today, squinting at Isobel from under her wide straw hat, she was silent.

Now the village cross came into sight. In the centre stood the war memorial with a low wall running round it. It was tea-time and Isobel was glad there was no-one about. She was even more glad she hadn't to go to Frank the grocer for messages. He was taking down his sun-blind. She hated the look of him with his green apron tied round his fat belly. When she asked for each item on her list he would repeat it after her, looking over the top of his glasses. 'Half a pound of butter'—pause—uh-huh and look. 'Half a dozen eggs'—pause—uh-huh and look. If there was a long pause before the uh-huh Isobel thought there must be a hidden meaning and would feel the heat spreading up her neck into her face. Today she was free of all that and she must get to the sweetie shop where she would leave her bike. In the corner of the window there was a notice in capital letters. On yellowed paper, the ink—faded to a faint brown—read:

> I AM MUCH OBLIGED IF CUSTOMERS
> WILL REFRAIN FROM PROPING THERE
> BIKES ON THE WINDOW AS IT CAUSES
> BAD DAMAGES THAT REQUIRE PAYING
> YOURS SINCERELY JANET McGOWAN

As Isobel re-read the notice she remembered Louise, her evacuee friend, and how they used to shout to one another,

'Louise, are you for "proping" your bike today?' or 'Isobel, be careful or Mrs McGowan will charge you for "proping"!' Shrieking, they would stagger about, holding each other up and laughing till they felt sick. But Louise had gone back to the city taking her laughter with her.

Obliging Mrs McGowan, Isobel propped her bike against the wall. She turned her back to the street and faced the window, knowing it was nearly time to begin. Suddenly he was there—between the pan drops and the jelly-babies. She swung round, fiddling with her hair, watching him through her moving fingers. He was almost at the corner. Swaying as he walked, he was whistling quietly, smiling to himself with half-closed eyes. Over his shoulder he had slung his chocolate brown tunic. In the sunshine Isobel noticed the glossiness of his black hair and the deep brown of his skin against his pale shirt. As he reached the corner at last, she took a deep breath. It was time to begin.

From behind her she heard a bike skidding to a stop.

'Hey, Izzy, Ah like the bike, where d'yi get this one eh?'

It was Roberta on her shining new bike. She drew alongside and rang Isobel's bell once, twice. Isobel clapped her hand over it, cutting off its ring.

'Knock, knock, Isobel. Say "Who's there?"'

Isobel glared at her.

'Izzy, say Isobel.'

Isobel looked past Roberta. It was time for Mario to move over to the war memorial.

'Isobel, is a bell on a bicycle—get it?'

Isobel shoved Roberta out of her way. Why was he not coming over? Instead he had turned at the corner and was facing Rita's chip shop doorway. Rita came out of the shop wearing her long white apron. Her thick red hair was loose on her shoulders and she had thrown her head back, laughing. With a great sweep of his arm Mario swung his tunic low across the pavement in front of her. Taking something from her apron she pushed it into Mario's shirt pocket. She patted his chest with both hands and he lightly touched her hair.

Her body shaking, Isobel rammed her fist against her teeth to keep the language of the farms from bursting out of her—Fat hooer 'n bitch frae hell—keechin' skite... She could hear the lorry labouring at the last hill. Mario was waving to Rita and sauntering over to the wall. Isobel began to walk towards him—there was still time. Wetting her lips she began to whistle but no sound came. She tried again and this time the sound came out clear and strong. Hear the music of the...

The lorry nosed into the cross, its engine roaring, belching out black smoke. From its open sides the Italian men caught sight of Rita and their roaring chorus of shouts drowned Isobel's sweet whistling. Mario was taking cigarettes from his shirt pocket and passing them round. As the lorry revved up to leave, the men lunged over to one side, waving and gesturing to Rita. She had taken off her apron and was waving them off, her white plump arms raised above her head.

In the silent and empty street the smell of the fumes lingered in the air. From the open door of the chip shop Rita began to sing in her low, rich voice:

*'One day when we were young*
*One wonderful morning in May*
*You told me you loved me*
*When we were young one day.'*

This was Rita's song that brought the house down at the village concerts. Everyone clapped and cheered and shouted Encore, Encore.

The farm boys at the back of the hall whistled through their thick fingers and hammered on the floor with their tacketty boots. Mr Gray, the hallkeeper, fearful of the damage to his new floor, would rush to the back to check them. For her encore she would sing, '*My luve's in Germanie, send him hame, send him hame*', and Isobel, hearing the sniffing and blowing on hankies, would shift in her seat. Mrs McLeod's sobbing had become so loud Mr Gray had had to take her outside.

At the sound of Rita's singing Isobel longed for Louise. She saw that her bike had slid down Mrs McGowan's wall, its wheels slowly ticking round. The blind in the sweetie shop was drawn now and as she went over to lift up her bike she caught sight of herself in the window. One of the legs of her shorts had unfolded and was flapping at her calf.

She yanked the bike on to its wheels with such force that as she dumped it down the bell rang spontaneously, a faint echo of its true sound. Roberta was calling to her. With her thin, bandy legs, arms outstretched, she was doing a balancing act along the memorial wall. In one hand she was pulling a yo-yo up and down. As Isobel watched Roberta wobbling, her skinny shape was blurring and flowing into the faded wreaths lying beneath the named men of the village.

'Isobel, seein' as yi hiv a bike the noo, are we gaun' tae the ferm the morrow?'

'Ah'll see, mibbe,' she called back.

As she passed Miss Turnbull's cottage she was glad there was no sign of her. Her deck chair, its canvas worn and faded, had been left out on the smooth lawn. Her black cat was asleep in a patch of evening sunshine. When she reached the farm gate again Isobel dragged herself over, then with the heel of her shoe hacked at a divot until it fell apart. She took the wilted primroses from her pocket and flung them into the hole. With first one foot and then the other she ground them back into the red earth. As she turned away the last lines of the song echoed in her head:

*'Then say not good-bye*

*Come back again beloved*

*Back to Sorrento*

*Or I must die.'*

From across the field a blackbird was starting up on a faraway tree, and as she listened Isobel knew that her song had come to an end.

# The Longest Day

**WHEN ISOBEL WAKENED** in the morning, the blackness of the night before had left her. It was going to be hot again and she felt cheerful at the thought of spending the day at Goodiebank farm.

They stood with their bikes ready to take the run down the brae.

'I'm goin' to keep my brakes off.'

'Naw Izzy, I wouldna dae that—remember what happened to…'

But Isobel was away.

'See you at the bottom.'

That was the trouble with Roberta, she believed every word you said. Isobel let the bike freewheel, braking at the first steep bend where wee Tommy had split his head open on the iron water trough. At Horses Grave she pulled hard on the brakes, remembering the coalman's horse that had to be put down. But worst of all was the stretch past the last corner where the doctor had stopped for his visit to the gatehouse. They said he had no lights on but Geordie the mechanic should never have been driving at yon speed, slamming into the back of the car and killing them both. On the last straight

Isobel slowed down at the empty lovers' seat and waited for Roberta. They pedalled easily across the flat carse roads. From the burnt grass verges rose puffs of dustiness mixed with the sickly sweet scent of the meadow-sweet. Rushing through warm then cool currents of air Isobel thought of the swimming in the loch. They turned up the loan to the farm and stopped at the gate into the hay field. The hay had been turned and dried and was ready for rucking. Resting in the shade of the hedge, the men were drinking from a can of sowans. At the sight of the girls one of them called out, laughing.

'Aye, aye—here the' come—the workers we cannae dae withoot. Whaur's yir forks lassies? We're near a' bye.'

Roberta's uncle Robert was staring at the cloudless sky, muttering, 'Aye, we'll pey for this, nae doot, nae doot.'

He had never forgotten the year of the drought when the corn stooks had stood in flooded fields till near November.

Bantum, the boy, was whistling through his teeth, practising his pipe tunes. To Isobel it was the sound of the curlews on the moors and she wished he would stop.

'Are ye for startin' then, lassies?'

'Naw, it's far too hot. We're away ti feed the calves. C'mon Izzy.'

Sometimes as they passed the henhouses, Auntie Chrissie would wave to them. Small and bent forward at the waist, she did everything at a half run. In her shredded red woollen hat, her pinny flapping, she looked, Isobel thought, like one of the hens she was feeding.

They left their bikes in the shed and went into the farm kitchen.

At the table Roberta's Auntie Chrissie and cousin Peggy were wrapping newly baked scones in a white cloth.

'Tak' a drink o' milk an' a scone. Is this no' some heat we're havin'? Peggy was fair done in oot in the field an' had tae come in tae change her cloth.'

Roberta snickered and nudged Isobel, who stared at her milk.

'Peggy's gaun tae the midsimmer dance in the hall the nicht. You twa isnae auld enough, but och, in a year or twa you'll baith hae lauds an' ye'll be fair ta'en awa wi' yersels. Wha's playin' the nicht? Is it Erchie and Company on the fiddles an' accordions?'

'Izzy's guid on the piano—sure y'are?'

Isobel pretended not to hear as Auntie Chrissie said, 'Hoo aboot ye gie us a wee tune then, whit d'ye say?'

Roberta egged her on.

'G'on Izzy, mind how yi played at ma birthday?'

'Play a tune for Mammy. Ye'll ken it fine—Wha saw the forty-second. Gae awa' ben to the piano in the parlour. Lea' the doors an' we'll can hear the soon' o't.'

Isobel walked slowly through to the parlour, which was sunless and cold. She sat down at the piano. A pale grey bloom of dampness covered its dark polished wood. In the brass candlestick holders were two half-burned candles. Their red wax had dripped onto the yellowed keys. Scored and chipped, many of them made no sound at all. On the top of the piano was a clutter of photographs in cardboard frames. One showed a heavy short legged bull with a rosette at its thick neck In another, a small smiling boy with white-blond hair was holding a Clydesdale horse. Underneath was printed one word: SUNSHINE. At the front of a family gathering, a fierce looking granny in a bonnet and old-fashioned clothes was holding a baby in a long white dress. A silver frame surrounded a young kilted soldier who seemed to be waiting for the command: 'At ease!' Under his tilted Glengarry his eyes looked straight at Isobel as she began to thump out his regimental march:

*'Wha saw the DUDty DUDond*

*Wha saw them DUD awa'*

*Wha saw the DUDty DUDond*

*Marchin' doon the DUDielaw.'*

Ashamed, she carried on, hearing a murmur of voices from the kitchen. And then there was silence, except for the slow ticking of a grandfather clock which stood in the corner of the room. Peggy was calling through.

'Come awa' ben, Isobel.'

She made her way back to the kitchen and at the sight of her face Peggy said, 'Dinnae tak' it on yersel' lassie. It wasnae your fau't.'

Auntie Chrissie was seated at the table where the scones lay in rows under the white cloth. Roberta, her mouth whitened with flour, was holding a half-eaten scone. She was staring at the floor. Tears lay on Peggy's sun-burned cheeks. Her rough reddened hand was laid on her mother's head. Its soft brown coil of hair had loosened and was straggling down her neck onto her shaking shoulders. Pressed to her face, the pink roses on her patterned apron had turned a dark crimson.

'Mammy'll be a' richt in a meenit. It jist cam' ower her

hearing Jamie's tune. It's near enough tae twa month that we kent he widnae be hame. C'mon Mammy, gae upstairs an' ha'e a wee lie doon on the tap o' the bed, an' ah'll get on wi' the milkin'.'

Outside in the late afternoon sun the cows in single file were slowly making their own way into the coolness of the byre. Their thin legs, easing past bulging udders, stepped daintily on their own skitters. Isobel thought of the bull calves she had fed that afternoon, their eyelashes smudged with milk. Often she had lain at night listening to the cows bellowing for their absent calves, knowing that in the morning she would see them dumped at the side of the road waiting to be collected, their heads sticking out of tied sacks.

'We'll no' bother wi' the milkin' the day, will we, Izzy?'

'No, no' the day.'

As they cycled back down the long farm road the hayfield was quiet. The men, finished with the rucking, had gone home for the night. Isobel remembered when Jamie had been put off the school bus for lighting papers. In his heavy farm boots, knees chafed raw above rumpled socks, he had kicked at stones at the side of the road. His leather helmet was flapping at the side of his purpling cheeks as he faced the long road home against the sleeting wind. The last time she had seen him was the day she was going to the pictures on the one o'clock Bluebird bus. He had got on at his road-end and at first she hadn't recognised him. His fair hair had been cut so that it looked like the stubble in the fields behind him. He was carrying a brown cardboard case and as the bus moved off he raised an arm in its stiff dark sleeve. They were waving from the field, leaning on their rakes and forks.

His father only turned his head and watched the bus disappearing, until it was a dot touching the edge of the sky.

They didn't speak much on the way home. The push up the brae seemed never-ending. When they reached the cross, Roberta turned off to go home.

'Whit aboot the loch the morrow, Izzy? It'll be warm.'

'I don't know, I'll see.'

She might not have the loan of the bike for another day.

Besides, she'd had enough of Roberta with her Izzy this and Izzy that. After her tea she would go and get cheered up at her Auntie Jean's. She always had time to stop for a cigarette and a blether. She might even have a new boarder.

Auntie Jean's kitchen was hot. She'd been baking oatcakes and they lay on a rack at the side of the range. Isobel put one on a plate and spread it with butter. The table was covered with layers of old blankets over which a white sheet was spread. Auntie Jean was using her new electric iron with the wooden handle that squeaked as it had done when Konrad was pressing his Air Force blue trousers at the same table. As the steam filled her nostrils Isobel could see him smiling at her, his eyes disappearing behind his high cheek bones. He didn't speak English and she watched him in silence. Carefully he had laid aside the iron. Putting his hands on her shoulders, he had kissed her on the lips, then laughing went back to his pressing, watching her through the steam.

'Which farm were you at today then?'

Auntie Jean was speaking.

'Goodiebank—the east side of Flanders Moss.'

Isobel began to tell her about Jamie. Her Auntie Jean looked out of the window. She drew her hand down a warm pillowcase, pressing and folding it against her body.

'Flanders Moss, yes of course—Flanders. Do you know your Uncle Will died in Flanders? He was only eighteen and was killed the week before the war ended—our wee brother. He was so innocent. I'm ironing here and remembering how he used to iron our girls' cloths. He didn't even know what they were. He was like that—just a boy.'

The oatcake in Isobel's mouth felt dry and tasteless. Auntie Jean, dipping her fingers into a bowl of water, carried on dampening the linen. As the flick, flick of the water darkened the pure white pillow case, so Isobel had watched her scarlet blood spattering on to the snow after the sledge had hurtled into the dyke at the bottom of the run.

'And now there's Konrad—what has become of him? It seems he's missing over Italy with his Polish squadron.'

Isobel took the last of her oatcake and slowly began to crumble it onto the plate until it was grey grit and dust. Auntie Jean's voice was sounding as if it was on the wireless but not right on the station.

'It's all such a waste—a terrible waste, but it'll be better for you, dearie. You're fair tired out looking. I think it's your bed you're needing.'

Isobel lifted her plate and laid it on the table beside the folded linen.

'Yes, I'll away—I'll be back up.'

She closed the door and walked out past the long shadows of the apple trees that had been in bud when Konrad had kissed her. She wanted to run but her body felt weighted and dead. The sentences in her head were broken, and the word *better* came stuttering in amongst them. From there, high up in the village she could see the carse now in shadow. The hills still had the evening sun on them and she named them as she had done since she first learned to speak. Ben Lomond, Ben Vorlich, Ben Ledi and Ben More. And what did this *better* mean? She thought then, the hills know nothing of better, they just are.

She walked past her own gate and headed up the hill. The dykes were still warm and she could smell the mix of scents from the warm moorland. High up on the last rise the sun was reddening the bark of the Scots pines. She lay on her face, shielding it with her arms, feeling the cool dampness of the sphagnum moss on her legs. From lower down the hill a thrush began singing from the top of a larch tree. As she sat up to listen she could make out the glimmer of its light speckled breast against the dark tree. She knew its pure song phrasing by heart. 'Did yi do it? Did yi do it?' And as she listened it changed in her ears until it was pouring out, 'You can do it. You can do it.'

She stood up and began to run down through the heather and the blaeberries. She tore through the waist-high bracken, across the rough field with the rashes at the burn. At home, in the long summer evening everyone was still out. She went through the dark house to the piano, and from the stool took out an old yellowed book: 'Songs from the Operettas'. She knew them all by heart and began to play her favourite. Closing her eyes, she stood up to sing.

*'Now or never, and for ever, I love you*

*Let me hold you till I've told you I love you*

*I believe in magic, while our arms entwine*

*Heaven's here when you are near, mine all mine.'*

She sang the last word and lifted the note to the octave above. As the sound throbbed in the top of her head she could feel her soreness floating away. When the note died there was no memory of Uncle Will or Jamie. And there was no Konrad. Gently she closed the piano, understanding the meaning of better.

# Mary Morison

**SHE IS SIXTEEN** years old and has been placed in the front row of the village choir. Most of the members are elderly. The tenor and bass voices wobble and crack and the sopranos produce a thin wailing sound. Only the mellow voices of the contraltos have not aged. As she listens to the simple four-part harmonies of the pieces they are rehearsing, she dreams of singing in vast echoing halls in faraway places. Their conductor is a plump, middle-aged widow. Wearing a tight black velvet dress, she will conduct their performance with vigorous enthusiasm. As she pivots on her mahogany podium (made for her by one of the basses) some of the audience will think to themselves that the swaying of her body is not quite decent. She has written a special arrangement of the Burns song *Mary Morison*.

The young tractor-man from one of the farms will sing the tenor solo and he is standing up preparing to sing. It is the same song she will sing the following evening at her school concert but her solo will have no elaborate arrangement. She watches the sheet of music fluttering in his trembling red hands and prays that tomorrow she will overcome her nervousness. The tenor is singing the opening lines and the basses will accompany him after the first verse:

*'Oh Mary, at thy window be,*
*It is the wish'd, thy trysted hour;*
*Those smiles and glances let me see...*

She is moved by the sweetness of his voice but it is the words which overwhelm her. For these are the 'smiles and glances' of her friend of the same name, Mary Morison, 'smiles and glances' which send Mary's teachers into a fury. They accuse her of silent insolence, disrespect and deceit. They shout at her that she is vain, shameful and ill-mannered. To all of these outbursts Mary takes a tortoiseshell comb from her blazer pocket and slowly draws it through the length of her waving auburn hair. Between finger and thumb she lifts a hair from her shoulder, adjusts her glasses with one finger, then tucks her smooth white blouse into her skirt under her full breasts. And it is this Mary Morison who has agreed to come from school for her tea before they return for their concert tomorrow evening.

The tenor, less nervous now, is floating a wordless, melodic line over the basses.

*'Yestreen when to the trembling string*
*The dance gaed thro 'the lighted ha'...'*

She thinks of the end of term dance, when Mary's neat feet and cool, steady hands will guide her through the St Bernard's Waltz.

*'I sigh'd, and said amang them a',*

*"Ye are na Mary Morison."'*

The men are singing softly; the conductor, her fingers on her lips, is shushing them down through the aching longing of the last line. As the voices die away there is the sudden sound of a door at the back of the hall being flung open, then slammed shut. The choir sit down, whispering amongst themselves, and the conductor carefully twists round on her podium. She is peering into the darkness where a man is moving forward, stumbling over the chairs. He is shouting, his slurred words echoing in the empty hall.

'I would say the tenor voice was perhaps flat... yes, flat... no, weak... yes, weak against the heavy bass line, and also, also if we consider what Burns is actually expressing... I mean, do we need this distraction, this embellishment? Oh yes, the Victorians knew how to kill Burns, didn't they? And here we have what amounts to...'

The light from the stage falls on him, revealing a handsome man, his dishevelled silver hair falling over his flushed face. Circling the air, wisps of smoke drift from his cigarette which he holds in long, fine fingers. He sways as he lifts his arms.

'Now, from the beginning.

*'O Mary, at thy window be.'*

His voice is neither a tenor nor a bass but a soft baritone, its timbre clouded by tobacco and alcohol. Knowing the man, the choir begins to mutter and whisper, some covering their mouths with their music. Their conductor, flushed and fidgety, steps down from her podium and has a word with the men. Two of them jump down from the stage and gently coax this intruder to the door. In the silence which follows the sharp closing of the door, his words, 'abysmal,' 'parochial' and 'cannot hold a candle to,' linger in the air.

No one refers to the interruption and soon the rehearsal is over. There is a shuffling of feet, gathering up of music, and their conductor hopes they will all be in good voice for their concert.

On her way home she half runs, pushing against a bitter north wind. She covers her mouth with her scarf, not wanting any throat trouble before she sings the following evening. She opens the back door, closes her eyes and stops to listen. In the scullery she slowly hangs up her coat, then carries her bag with the music in it into the warm kitchen. Her mother, smiling, turns to her. Holding a large brown teapot, she asks how the practice went, and would she like some tea and toast. She makes no reply, staring at her father seated at the table resting his head on his hands. She can feel the blood draining from her face and there is a humming in her ears. She hurls her bag across the kitchen. It slams against the door of the dresser, making the plates rock and the cups dance on their hooks. Her fists clenched, she moves across to her father, circling him, looking down at his bent head. The words choke in her raw, tight throat. She screams of her shame at the state of him, the sight of him in the hall and the spoiling of everything. Finally she spits out at him that if he is in the gutter, why doesn't he disappear down a drain!

Suddenly he stands up. With one hand he lifts his chair

above his head, then swings it down, sweeping everything from the table. On the linoleum floor his half-eaten supper lies strewn amongst the broken crockery, and cold tea dribbles slowly down the thin, flowered curtain. Torn by the jagged glass of the broken window, it flaps in the cold night air. She looks at the white splintered wood of the delicate Bentwood chair and remembers how she used to push her small fingers through the holes of the seat, counting them one by one.

When the rising voices have died down she sleeps, dreaming that Mary is seated at the kitchen table. Her mother is serving her a plate piled high with broken glass and old scraps of food. In the morning her mother looks ill and exhausted. More than once she asks her mother if she is remembering Mary is coming tonight.

The school day drags past but now Mary is here at last. She is here—here in the kitchen. Her mother has tidied, and smoothed her hair across her brow, and is hanging Mary's coat on a peg on the door. She is telling them they haven't much time, and will sausages be all right? She has seated Mary with her back to the window, over which a piece of cardboard has been nailed.

She watches Mary cutting her sausages into small pieces. One by one, from the end of her fork, she places them delicately between her lips. She is holding her knife the same way as she holds her pen in class, her elbow tucked in at her side, and every so often she shakes back her auburn hair and adjusts her glasses. Too soon her mother is helping them into their coats, telling her to sing well, and to wrap up as there is snow in the wind. As they run to catch the bus in the fading light a few flakes of snow are beginning to settle.

Not far from the school where his daughter is about to sing, a man has bought a book of Burns' songs. It is nearly closing time in the music shop and he is detaining the assistant who is listening patiently to his repeated and lengthy interpretation of an engraving reproduced on the frontispiece.

'POST CINERIS GLORIA VENIT.' He announces each word precisely. Does she know Latin? Does she understand what that means?

'The meaning, of course... Ah, the meaning...' He sighs deeply.

'Yes, well. Post cineris gloria venit. Glory comes after death.'

He snorts, and she can smell the whisky on his breath.

'Here, you see, is cant... hypocrisy... do you understand? Well, Burns wrote about it, didn't he? And, of course, here we have music, the daisy, the plough, all symbols from his poems, and here the Bible he gave to Highland Mary. Ah, Mary! Yes, Mary. Now... Mary Morison.' He pauses.

'Yes, it is a tenor song, but never mind. She has a rare voice, a very rare voice. Did I mention my daughter's voice? Did I mention that?'

The assistant lifts the keys from the counter and says she really must close now. She places the music book in a brown paper bag which he tucks under his arm as he steps into the dark street.

Outside in the thickening snow as he fumbles over the lighting of his cigarette, the music tumbles from the paper bag and slides across the slushy pavement. Leaning over to pick it up, his feet slither under him. Somebody steadies him and hands him the soaking book. As he drags his sleeve across the cover he calls after the disappearing figure that she's only sixteen.

'You know... given time... given the training... deserves the best... you hear... only the best for such a voice...'

And with the snow now settling on his bare head and shoulders he suddenly stands up straight. From the fankled line of the song in his head, he sings in full voice to the hushed and empty street.

*'If love for love thou wilt na gie,*
*At least be pity to me shown...'*

And then, his head sinking down to his chest, he mumbles:

*'I sigh'd and said amang them a'*
*"Ye are na Mary Morison."'*

At the school concert the audience are not seated in a hall but jammed between white scrubbed wooden tables and the deep china sinks in the cookery room. To calm her nerves as she prepares to sing her solo, she counts the crisp white dish towels hanging on the pulleys, and reads the ingredients for Semolina Snow written in white chalk on the blackboard. A strong smell of soap fills her nostrils as she breathes in before singing the opening line: *Oh Mary, at thy window be...*

She looks over to where Mary is seated. She has taken a

tortoiseshell comb from her pocket and is slowly combing her hair, gazing dreamily out of the window into the dark night where it is snowing steadily.

# Displaced Person

**ELMA GRANT**—Miss Elma Grant., teacher of art, stood at her classroom door waiting for her class. Framed in the doorway, she had the tall fair grace of a Botticelli painting. It was Friday, 1.30 p.m. There would be precisely 2 hours and 15 minutes before she gained her release. She checked her watch with the clock at the end of the dingy corridor. On the walls hung faded prints of saints, their eyes casting up to heaven. Round these haloed figures with drooping heads, pneumatic cherubs winged effortlessly. A placid infant Jesus, with rouged cheeks, nestled on the breast of his eternally adoring mother. In her Presbyterian upbringing amongst farming folk there had been a bleak absence of all decoration in the small stone churches. School corridors were bare. No prayers were offered up to comforting saints, no confessional to soften the sin, only the awesome hard space between herself and God. The folks she grew up with were at best douce, at worst dour and unco guid. She could see her class spilling out from the stairwell, jostling with one another in the narrow corridor. The girls were rushing ahead, eager to be first into the classroom. Behind them the boys grappled with one another, taking wild swipes with their bags. Miss Grant raised her eyes towards a stucco figure of

Christ, his precious raspberry-coloured blood spilling onto his milk-while body and limbs. 'Dear Lord,' she prayed, 'let Giorgio Bonaldi be absent today.'

There was a high screeching from Anne Marie, her thin white face full of venom.

'Hey—watch it—that's ma cookin' yir huttin'.'

'Gonny gie iz some but?' Big Patrick McGowan stabbed a dirty forefinger at her pie dish full of mashed potato.

'Don' ack i' Gownsy—Miss, can ah gi'in tae pi' this oo' o' his road?'

Miss Grant sighed and unlocked the door.

'Take out your folders—and jackets off—all of them.'

This wasn't the worst of her classes. They would settle down eventually—except of course for Mr Bonaldi. Where was he anyway? Casually she asked the class, 'Is Giorgio Bonaldi here today?'

Anne Marie piped up, 'Oh aye, Miss. He had tae go and ge' lines for flingin' potatoes in the dinner hall.'

Her heart sank—there would be no respite today then.

The wet jackets heaped up on the top of the side cupboards gave off a sour smell mixed with that of the mashed potato pies placed for safety on top of a cupboard behind her table.

'Right, have you all found your folders? Gerard, what's wrong?' A shilpit wee soul, he reminded her of a gerbil. He had sandy coloured hair, pale eyes and his tiny hands were perfectly formed.

'Ah cunny fin' ma folder,' he squeaked.

'Have you looked in the other shelves? Come on, we have this performance every week—we haven't...'

The door burst open. Giorgio Bonaldi had arrived. He crashed the door behind him, flung his bag to the floor, and spread his arms out wide.

'*Ta-rah*—Ah'm here Miss.'

'Right, we can all see that. Just find your work and get started.'

'No' draw the day—Eh?—how no'?'

'Remember we finished our drawing module last week and I went over the design lesson we will all begin today.'

'No' me Miss—Ah'm gonny pose again.'

At that he tossed his jacket over to the side cupboard and stripped off his jersey. Carefully folding it into a cushion, he laid it on the floor.

'Giorgio, you don't seem to have heard—I said—'

'Ow abou' *iss* Miss—*owza'* eh?'

He lay down on the floor, supporting his head with his left hand, elbow resting on his prepared cushion. He raised his right knee; the left leg, slightly bent, lay along the floor. He was totally relaxed.

At each lesson last week she had remonstrated with him, insisting he could not be the only model. And here he was going through his routine again. She could feel her anger rising. His arrogant self-confidence contrasted with the immaturity of the other boys. He was physically years ahead of them and he knew it. The strong features of his head had a sculptural quality: a Donatello's David. His body, its dark golden skin contrasting with the white shirt, called out to be painted.

'The cheek of him—the sheer cheek,' she thought. She would have to get him off the floor—but how? Now the comments had begun—'Luk a' him. Thinks he's I.T.'—

'Fancies hissel'— 'Big heid—watch it disnae fa' aff'— 'Miss, get his stinkin' feet away fae ma table'—'Miss, how come he's lyin' on the flair—see if i' wis ony uz, we'd get…'

'Right class, that's enough. I suggest we ignore glamorous Giorgio.'

Perhaps sarcasm would shame him. But he smiled slyly, closed his eyes and settled down more comfortably.

'Just leave him,' she thought. 'Ignore him.'

The class quietened down, but there was a sudden bawling from next door.

Oh dear, here we go, another rough afternoon for John McCann with his French class. He was shouting over the rumpus that had erupted—

*'Toujours la politesse.'*

*'Toujours la politesse'* echoed in her ears. She was standing looking out of the window overlooking the school car park. Two men were digging up the shrubs from the banking. As they hauled them out from the red earth, stones scuttered down like potatoes freed from their shaws. 'Required too much maintenance,' so they said. The warm afternoon sun had cleared the autumn mist and a slanting light filled the classroom. It touched Giorgio's reclining figure, illuminating him like a fragment of an Italian fresco. Someone had decorated his boots with scraps of yellow paper. She became overwhelmed with the feeling that this day was like a misaligned print in a repeat pattern, the design now askew, the images blurred. On that other day, she was fourteen years old and her school was on holiday for the potato harvesting. She had joined the other children on the bus and would soon be tattie howkin' on one of the arable

farms. It was set on the edge of the carse, on an ancient raised beach. The farmer was known as Gibby, The Shore. Years of keeping an eye on the weather had turned him into a silent, bad-tempered man. That morning the October mist lying over the carse had become a sea out of which the hills rose up, transformed into distant islands. The bus sailed through an oak forest, the trees dripping with water.

The morning's work began as usual with the grieve hammering in pegs to mark off the stents in the drills. Besides the squad of schoolchildren there were some displaced persons from the camp—or DPS as they were called. The DPS were different from the other prisoners of war who worked on the farms. They had none of the cheerful bravado of the Italians or the restraint of the Germans. The locals found their language incomprehensible and the whereabouts of their homelands a great mystery. As they worked Gibby the farmer passed up and down the road in his horse-drawn cart. When they stopped to rest he would shout, 'Get yer backs intae it! That's stealt time, come on, back doon tae it.'

The soaking mist had lifted and they had dried out in the warm sun. The boys were growing bored and were looking for stinking rotten potatoes to fling at each other. One flew through the air and caught one of the DPS as he straightened up, splattering his thick-lensed glasses. He removed them slowly, wiping them carefully on the sleeve of his khaki greatcoat. In a low clear voice he said, 'Boys—*toujours la politesse.*' She knew what it meant, but the boys sniggered and looked shamefaced. Gibby was passing on his cart, heading up to the farm again. He was standing with one arm holding the slack of his horse's reins, his other arm raised with his fist clenched. His angry shouting drifted away on the wind. 'Waste, wasting ... wait till…'

They bent down to gather the last of the potatoes, their backs aching, wishing it was time to go home. And then the grieve was running up the drills towards them, agitated and waving his arms.

'Get the hale place redd-up—Gibby's deid!'

They all stood still, not understanding, and then a feeling of guilt overcame them. They must have been the cause of first his anger and then his death. They straggled down the field to wait for the bus. The DP was sitting leaning against a fence, reading a book, shut off from all the commotion.

As she passed the grieve he was shouting, 'At the tap o' the stack—fell doon like a stane!'

She must collect her coat from the farmhouse and make her way past the stackyard. The back door was wide open; some hens were pecking at the step. She went in awkwardly through the ice-cold dairy into the kitchen, which was empty and silent. To get to the parlour she had to pass through the lobby where the aspidistra plants sat in large patterned china pots. The parlour door was closed. She grasped the brass handle, slowly opened it, and was met with the strong musty smell of the unused room. Between the dark polished legs of the furniture Gibby was stretched out on the patterned linoleum. His old face was stone white, his dark blue jacket and trousers as she'd last seen them when he shook his fist. His huge tacketty boots, caked with mud and straw from the stackyard, were pointing up to the ceiling. As she reached across him to gather up her coat from the black horse-hair sofa she was filled with horror and a deep sense of wrong-doing.

* * *

'In the name of the Father, the Son, and the Holy Ghost, Amen.' The class had cleared up and were finishing their prayer. The floor where Giorgio had lain was sunless and bare. There was no sign of him.

'Miss, we've said wir prayer. Gonny le' us ou' before the bell, gonny no' keep us?'

Gerard, distressed, was clutching his drawing, pleading in his high voice, 'Miss, ah canny fin' ma folder an'iss is ma bess drawn. Wanny no' loss it.'

'Oh, just leave it, Gerard. I'll put it away safely.'

The bell rang and the class rushed out, clutching jackets, mashed potato pies, and bags.

In the peaceful silence she looked at Gerard's drawing. He had ignored the new design lesson and had drawn a reclining figure. With the finest lines he had captured the relaxed beauty of Giorgio's pose. Every detail had been painstakingly recorded, from the curl of his hair to the scraps of paper which decorated the boots. Underneath was printed in large capital letters:

HERE LIES GIORGIO BONALDI
DIED OCTOBER 10
R.I.P.
BY GERARD McCAFFERTY

# The Class

**AS SHE PUSHES** open the heavy library door Mrs Telfer can smell the hot over-used air. She hopes they will open a window. In a small area to the side of the library about a dozen chairs have been placed in two rows. On a stand facing the chairs a large flip-chart has been placed. At the sight of it Mrs Telfer's heart sinks. She hates them. Some others begin to arrive. There is a woman with glasses on a gold chain, and a young, plump, dark woman. A confident, stocky man gives the impression that this class in T.V. script-writing is all in the day's work. Two men come in together. The younger man, dark and serious, wears glasses. The older man is wearing the kind of outfit men used to wear—a coat and hat. No-one speaks. The chairs scrape as they sit down, and then the young woman with the chained glasses announces that she used to clean lavatories and now earns her living writing for television. Everyone is silently impressed. There is a flurry at the door, and the spinsterish librarian, flushed and chattery, is ushering in a young man. Mrs Telfer sums him up in one word. Sexy. She is aware that this word is the current word to describe music, theatre, art, and even places. But right now she knows the word to be correct. He places his legs apart and rocks to and fro on his thick-soled suede shoes. The chunky look, she thinks. Hunk. Chunky. He is speaking. She must concentrate.

'Hi! I'm Kev. Tonight we are going to write a script for a T.V. soap. Of course, we won't finish it tonight.' People smile. 'But give us a week or two and we'll have it slung together.'

'Now—let me say this straight away, and I can't say this any stronger. I am sick, sick of the fuckin' middle class writing for working-class soaps!'

There is silence. The coat and hat man has taken off his hat, and coughs. Mrs Telfer wishes she hadn't sat in the front row. She looks down at her leather court shoes and her tartan skirt. She flushes, aware of her Balmoral appearance. She knows that an assumption will have been made, that she appears prim, precious, and, worst of all, limited. The gibe at the middle class has struck home, making her feel confused and guilty of her appreciation of everything that was opened up to her through her education. And then she remembers her uncle with his collection of opera records, his books, his love of paintings. And he worked all his life in heavy industry. She wants to stand up, shout, demand an explanation of his definition of class, but she sits in silence, choked with anger. Kev is shouting now. She wonders why he is shouting at all six of them. Any minute now that terrifying maths teacher will hit her on the back of the head, roaring that of course the point would move to the left and not to the right.

'Give me a character,' Kev is shouting. 'Quick! Off the top of your head.'

He is pointing his pen straight at her. She feels the maths class brain-freeze coming on, and then she thinks of her friend's son with his degree in philosophy, working as a bouncer at a night-club. She disguises his name and says, 'Leonard.'

His pen at the ready, Kev says, 'What is he?'

'A bouncer.'

'Great! Any more? Come on—'

The confident man is saying:

'Ah grew up in a tenement an ah've saw the whole a'life there, so ah'm gonny gie yi this guy, Dave. He wis an alchy yi know, but noo he's dried oot an—'

'Aw, terrific!' says Kev. He writes up Dave in large capital letters.

The serious young man at the back says in a quiet voice:

'A poacher.'

'A poacher?' asks Kev.

'Yes, a poacher.'

'Of women?' asks Kev, his voice rising.

'*No,* animals.'

'Animals? What's his name?'

'Gunner.'

'Gunner?'

'Yes, Gunner.'

Kev writes up Gunner, in small letters.

'Okay. We need a woman.'

'Theresa,' says the T.V. scriptwriter.

'Uhhuh?' Kev winks at her. 'You've been at this before—and?'

'She's a drug addict, has two kids to support, and is

trying to—'

Tenement man breaks in:

'An' her an' Big Joss, he's a dealer an' he's in the hoose when—'

Big Joss and Theresa are both written up in giant capital letters.

'Okay,' says Kev. 'What a beginning! Great stuff. Great characters. Now *connect.* Set the scene. Okay. You've got fifteen minutes, and mind, no stories, and no conferring!'

He and the script-writer disappear behind the library book shelving. There is silence. The young plump woman is yawning, doodling on a piece of paper. The men are writing as if it is an examination. Suddenly the young woman stands up.

'I think I'll go home. I've no idea what to write.'

Kev looks over the book shelf and shouts:

'I said no conferring!'

The young man flings down his pencil. Mrs Telfer writes a list of words. Conflict. Poverty. Boredom. Beer cans. Cigarette stubs. Drug addiction. Prostitution.

'Time's up.'

Kev is back.

He fires at Mrs Telfer first, black pen like a pistol.

'The scene?'

She reads her effort and at 'drug addiction'. Kev interrupts:

'Spot on. Brilliant. You?'

He stabs his pen at the coat and hat man, who reads from a closely-written paper what to Mrs Telfer's ears is a beautifully crafted piece of descriptive writing. He has read only two lines when Kev shouts:

'I said, no fuckin' stories. Remember?'

No-one moves. Mrs Telfer's heart goes out to the would-be writer.

'So, you?'

The tenement man says:

'Well, the man that wis oan the booze has turned up at his pal's and Big Mac that's wi' him—'

Kev writes up Big Mac.

'He's wantin' a fight 'cos he hisnae forgot aboot the money he owes—'

Kev interrupts:

'And he jumps in and sticks one on him that was his pal, and the other one that was on the booze is batterin' in at him, and Theresa, that's on the sofa, thinks her boyfriend Joey is goin' tae-'

He turns to his chart, the pen squeaking as the black lines zigzag from name to name. In the blizzard of lines Mrs Telfer has lost sight of her Leonard. The heat is making her feel faint, and she longs to be away from this chaos.

And then Kev is telling them that as they've worked so hard, he'll let them go early, but to write it up for next week.

'Remember,' he says. 'Keep it tight. No novels.'

Outside in the fresh air Mrs Telfer stops to button her coat. The serious young man steps forward and asks if she is all right, saying he is appalled and angry at the language. She shrugs and says it was his remark about the middle class which upset her more than the swearing. His friend joins them, laughing.

'What's so funny?' asks the younger man.

'It's just—did you see the tattoo on his arm?'

'Yes. What did it say?

'Know what it said? It said *Kev.* Just *Kev.*'

Together they walk down the street, helpless with laughter.

When Mrs Telfer arrives home she pauses in front of her hall mirror. She looks at her white-haired reflection and says, 'You're just a middle-class sheep', and walks away. And then she turns back, peers into the mirror again and says, 'Correction. Fucking middle-class sheep.'

# Safety

**'ROBERT**, you're not listening!'

'I am, Janet, I am!'

'No, you're not. You're doing your usual, whenever there's something to discuss, you...'

He slowly lowered his newspaper.

'Okay. What is it?'

'We'll have to do something about a side gate. Alan's climbing up onto everything and you promised you'd get started on a side fence. But when? Are you going to wait till... till... Look, I heard you can pick up an old door down the town where they're demolishing the buildings.'

'You couldn't carry a door. Just leave it to me.'

'No, I'll go down and check if it's okay. I'll go tomorrow, right? Aileen next door will look after Alan.'

In the morning she left the baby with her neighbour and set out on her bike. She would be down at the site in no time. She took the path alongside the high convent wall and the Catholic school; then down the brae at the Royal Academy which stood high, overlooking the Low Green and Waterside.

She turned at Seagate Castle and pedalled easily up West

Road where she passed a stout priest slowly making his way to the Chapel.

Pushing her bike through the close she came out opposite Trinity Church. Now she would have to find someone who would give her access to the demolition site on the other side of the river.

As she propped her bike against the railings at the church she saw that some of the men had come up from the site at Cochrane Street and were lounging on the grass in front of the church. Most of them were stripped to the waist.

'Excuse me, could you tell me where I would find the boss?'

There was a roar of laughter.

'Darlin', we're a' bosses! Hey, Gammy, hoo aboot you, eh?'

'Maybe ye'd like tae speak tae me—you and me—the baith o' us!'

'Hello, here's Picasso—he'll see tae ye. Right, Picasso boy, you'll see tae the lady—nae bother!'

A tall figure lifted himself up, leaned on his elbows and said, 'Can I help you? Is there something you want to see in the church? It's not open.'

'No, it's nothing to do with the church. I'm looking for a door.'

The men started up again.

'A door, hen? A hingin' door? A back door? A front door? A lavvy door? We hae a' kinds o' doors—doon there across the bridge!'

Picasso opened the gate and lifted her bike.

'Here, come with me. I'll show you.'

'Aye, see and show her, Picasso, eh? Mind we start up in ten minutes. Will that be enough time?'

Ignoring them he wheeled her bike along the pavement, apologising to someone who was nearly clipped by the pedal.

'So... how come you're looking for a door, then?'

She explained briefly about the need to provide a safe place for the baby.

He pointed to where the smoke was rising. The burning of the wood from the old buildings.

'It's tragic!'

'What?'

'I'm saying it's tragic; lovely old buildings, torn down for what? Some concrete shopping mall. Look, see over at Loudon Street? That was my primary school—gone—and my next school, Loudon Montgomerie—they're putting a huge roundabout there—destroying a wonderful Victorian building; beautiful wood, brass fittings... all to be bulldozed!'

'You come from Irvine, then?'

'Och, aye, but I'll be glad to be shot of the place. This is my summer job. I'm doing sculpture at the Glasgow School of Art.'

'Is that why they call you Picasso?'

'Aye! It's the only artist's name they know. But, they're a good bunch of lads.'

'You're a bit older than some...'

'Yes, I'm a late beginner; worked around; travelled down south and now I'm working on a big piece for the church—a Mother and Child. I've got the use of the yard at the monumental sculptors—Axford's—until it's bulldozed as well.'

They had reached a half demolished building.

'This was the sweetie shop where I got my comics, and next door was the music shop, with a piano in the window. You wouldn't know it—you don't come from here, do you?'

'No, I'm from up north. We had Alan christened in the Fullerton Church, just there.'

She pointed to the church, its gates closed and locked.

He laid her bike against the crumbling door jam and held her elbow, telling her to watch her feet. In the dark interior she made out various doors leaning against the wall.

Chipped and scored, they revealed how, over the years, different colours had been painted one upon the other. Hanging in grotesque strips, layer upon layer or various patterned wallpapers were peeling down the old, damp, plaster walls.

'It's sad, isn't it? Families lived here. Generations cosied round that fireplace. Look, there's even an old, black kettle.'

He picked it up and turned it over, silently feeling the curve of the spout.

'Here, hold it; it's beautiful'

She stepped towards him and lost her balance on one of the exposed joists. He dropped the kettle and steadied her with his body, his arms around her back.

When he kissed her mouth she smelled the dustiness of the old plaster on his shirt mixed with the wood smoke in his hair.

He drew away and touched her face lightly. Then, cupping his hand, he drew it over her head, across the nape of her neck, onto her shoulders and across her breast. He spoke softly. 'This is where I am struggling with my piece, this beautiful line here.'

He was silhouetted against the gaping window. A shaft of sunlight lit up the red-gold hair waving over his neck almost to his shoulders. He had a puzzling familiarity, but she could not think of whom or where. And then she saw the figure with outstretched arms. 'Suffer little children to come unto me…' It was the figure in the stained glass window of the church where their baby had been Christened.

There was the sound of an engine starting up. A man laughed and shouted, 'Hey, Picasso! Time's up!'

He moved away from her, calling out, 'Aye! I'm in here! So—that door there, then? That's a good door. It'll clean up fine. Three five Kilwinning Road, you said?'

Unable to meet his eyes, she felt her neck and cheeks flush and remained silent.

'I'll bring it up in the morning. Right. See you then.'

And he was away, striding back over the bridge, whistling in time to his steps.

Not wanting to face the men again she decided to go back along Waterside. As she cycled past Friar's Croft the smoke from the bonfires stung her eyes. She dismounted at the footbridge over the river, then cycled up the path across from the Fire Station. At the slight rise by the Royal Academy her legs felt weak and she was glad of the level ground at the statue of Robert Bums. She was nearly home.

That evening Janet was relieved that Robert was preoccupied writing up the minutes for a meeting at the golf club. He had said it was good that she had arranged for the delivery of the door, assuring her repeatedly that he would get started on the side fence as soon as possible.

The next morning Janet was restless and short with the

baby. At midday there was a loud thumping on the back door. Hastily, she lifted the baby and put him in his play-pen, trying to calm herself.

When she opened the door two grinning lads were standing, one on each side of a scuffed door.

'Got ye in a oner! Three five, no bad, eh? Oh, by the way, Picasso's gone walkabout! Somebody seen'im getting on the train— 'way back tae London, nae doot! Naw, naw, ye don't owe us nuthin'. Ta-ra!'

She closed the door and went through to where she'd left the baby. On tiptoe he eagerly stretched up his arms. She lifted him up and nestled into the sweet smell of the soft curled hair on his neck. She carried him to the window and, through her tears, murmured, 'We're safe—both safe.'

# Icarus

**SHE SETTLES HERSELF** on the warm wooden seat of the swing and feels the cold chains against her bare arms. She begins to rock gently. 'Good,' she thinks, 'the toughies are running away. It's safe now.' Just the way they stared at her made her feel scared.

They always want the swing you are on, shouting, 'Want a jeely nose, eh?' But the worst is at the top of the chute. If you stop, thinking it might be too steep, they begin shoving and punching your back till you have to let go, with them screaming, 'Feartie-feartie!' And if she had her kilt on, 'Kilty, kilty cauld bum, you're for it!'

But today is different.

Just remember how to make the swing work up. 'Legs out straight,' her mother said. 'Lean forward, pull back, with strong straight arms—and again. Tuck your legs in—again… You can do it… Now you've got it!'

Yes, it's working; she'd got the rhythm. The sweep of the chains is long and slow, not like the ones at home that jerked and squeaked. Now she can rest and dream. The air feels warm on her arms and legs. She closes her eyes against the brightness of the sun.

'Never look at the sun,' her mother said. She never forgot that but what was the name of the man in that story, who was flying too high, near the sun? Maybe he'd felt good like this before he fell. She wouldn't do that, not after what happened to yon boy who went right over the bar and had to be taken to hospital.

She didn't think the man who fell out of the sky went to hospital. Maybe he went into a spin like when planes crash, or did he just go straight down and land with a thump, like Mrs Davy's wee boy that was stealing apples and fell and broke his back? They said his mother went mental after it.

What was it the teacher had said about the man's wings? 'Children, his wings weren't strong enough to stand the heat and they melted. Now then, what have we learned from our story today? Yes?'

'Never to go too near a hot fire,' said someone, and then Andy Brown said, 'Miss, I havenae goat ony wings,' and the teacher told him to sit down and be quiet. He had matches taken off him the day before and got four of the belt. The teacher called him a troublemaker. The man in the sky had trouble all right! Did he not think something terrible could happen, or did he not know how to make strong wings?

Right enough, wings are hard to make. *She* knows that. The ones her mother helped to make for the Christmas play fell to bits the first time she put them on. And Theresa, her that was Mary, had laughed, pointing at the shredded paper hanging from her back.

That's just what happened to *his* wings as well because when the teacher finished the story, she turned the book round and we could all see the picture. Sure enough, there he was, with a terrible sad face. But his wings were not made of white-painted newspaper. They were pure shining gold, splintering like her stick of rock when it broke into a hundred bits against the stone shed, and she couldn't catch one of them.

She opens her eyes. The sun is low behind the trees and she is dying down. She begins to sing to herself,

*'Rocking down, dropping down,*

*Over the town, Like a dying clown...'*

Someone is shouting. 'Oh no, please, not those toughies back again!'

She looks down. Two small children are looking up. 'We got tired waiting and waiting for you, so we went and got ice-cream. Can we go home now, Granny?'

CPSIA information can be obtained at www.ICGtesting.com
Printed in the USA
BVOW01s1416160514

353759BV00001B/23/P

9 781908 026385